SISTERS OF THE SEA

CONNECTED THROUGH BRAVERY, DETERMINATION, AND KINDNESS

BY

ANNABELLE J. REEVES

DEBORAH J. REEVES

TABLE OF CONTENTS

DEDICATION PAGE

To my Granddaughter Annabelle,

Your imagination flows as deep as the sea and shines as bright as the stars. You carry magic, kindness, and wonder wherever you go. Thank you, Belle, for letting me dive into your imagination. Never stop creating and always make room for your dreams.

Your-Co-creator

Toto Debbie

To every person holding this book,

This story began with a 6-year-old girl and an imagination as wide as the ocean. This book serves as a reminder that even the smallest voices can create big waves. Know in your heart you are brave, kind, perfect exactly as you are, and full of magical wonder. Continue to dance, dream, and never stop imagining, no matter your age. The magical sea is big enough for all of us.

Annabelle and Toto Debbie

Beneath the sparkling waves, where sunlight shimmered like golden treasure, lived two sisters who loved each other more than anything. But with so much sea between them, even the closest hearts can sometimes feel distant. The oldest was born under a silver moon, the sea whispering lullabies as cool water held her close. The youngest arrived with the rising sun, warm light dancing on her cheeks as bubbly waves sparkled around her.

The moon-born sister lived where dark waters whispered through the night. The sun-born sister danced where bright waves sang in the light. Neither realized that the ocean's call would someday bring them together, forever changing their hearts and lives.

In the deep, dreamy sea, the oldest sister, Vampire, lived where moonlight spilled like silver glitter. The creatures called her Shadow Dancer, for she moved so softly even the tiniest shrimp never saw her. She twirled through drifting seaweed, humming lullabies to the stars, her heart glowing brighter than the lanternfish who lit her way.

Her younger sister, Queen, was just as beautiful. The sea called her the Light Dancer, for she sparkled like sunlight on coral and laughed like the bubbles that raced to the surface. From morning to night, she twirled through glistening waves, her tail flashing colors brighter than a rainbow reef. Wherever she danced, schools of fish followed, weaving like part of her song.

Queen loved to dance. If she stumbled, she would giggle, she would flip her fins, and try again—because only the most joyful, graceful dancer could wear the royal coral crown. Every day she practiced with dolphins, while anemones clapped, and turtles tapped along to her shimmering sea-song.

But one warm, golden evening, just as the sun began to sink into the ocean, something strange happened. Queen was twirling just under the surface when— *flip*— her tail splashed up through the waves, pointing straight at the glowing sun. Her fins shimmered like magic… and then—they turned into feet!

Queen gasped. "What's happening?!" She kicked, but without her tail, she could no longer swim. The water pulled at her like a swirling whirlpool. "I cannot swim! I cannot breathe!" she cried. A single shiny tear, bright as a pearl, slipped down her cheek and floated to the ocean floor.

Far below, in the shadowy deep sea, Vampire felt her sister's fear ripple through the water. She rushed upward to save her sister, hair streaming like silken ribbons, eyes glowing with determination. In a heartbeat, she reached Queen, holding her tight. "I have you, little sister. I am here. You are safe," she whispered, her voice calm and steady as the tide.

The ocean grew still. Even the waves held their breath. And in that quiet moment, the sisters' hearts beat together again, bound by bravery, determination, love, and the magic of finding each other.

Using the magic of the ocean, the sisters began to make a special healing potion. They added Queen's fallen tear, a ribbon of moonlight caught in the waves by a playful dolphin, and a tiny star-shaped shell that a sea turtle carried from the sandy floor. They mixed in shimmering bubbles made by a school of silverfish spinning in happy circles, glowing petals from moon coral, fresh seagrass brought by a gentle eel, and the magical power of the mermaids' song as they sang their wishes.

The potion sparkled with a thousand colors. Then—POOF! — Queen's beautiful tail returned! The sisters hugged tight, hearts brimming with joy. It felt as though the whole ocean wrapped around them, holding them safe and close in a friendly embrace.

From that day on, they promised never to let the ocean's miles pull them apart again. They found the perfect place for them, a coral castle halfway between light and shadow. Not too bright, not too dark- perfect. There, they swam together, dreamed together, and created new dances every single day and night.

Then came the day of the Summer Pageant—the most magical celebration in all the sea. Queen twirled with excitement as she practiced her dances. But this year, she was not the only one ready to dance. For the very first time, Vampire entered the pageant… and the ocean buzzed with surprise.

Fish, eels, whales, crabs, octopuses, dolphins, sea turtles, sea dragons, and mermaids all turned to stare.

"The Shadow Dancer?"

"The mermaid of the deep?" they whispered.

The music began, and Vampire stepped onto the coral stage. Then—magic. She moved like the night sky dancing with the stars, graceful, powerful, and full of mystery. Every spin, every flip told a story—their story—of shadows and light, of sisters finding each other again through love.

When the last pearl drifted down, the crowd grew silent… and then burst into the loudest cheer the sea had ever heard! Vampire had won the crown.

No one cheered louder than Queen. With eyes shining like sunlight on water, she placed the shimmering coral crown on her sister's head and laughed with joy. "The sea is big enough for both our dreams," she said. And as they hugged, it felt like the whole sea was hugging them and that the crown did not just belong to the winner—it belonged to them both.

From that day on, the mermaid sisters— one of shadow, one of light—ruled the sea. Under the sun and the moon, they danced together, their tails swirling like ribbons in the water. They showed all the sea creatures that everyone shines in their unique way. They taught that true strength grows when you face your fears together, stay focused on what you want, celebrate what makes each other different, and share kindness in a world that is big enough for all of us.

Moonbeams dance on the deep, deep sea,

Sunshine sparkles on coral bright,

Together we shine in the ocean's light...

Connected through bravery, determination, and kindness.

VIDEO TRAILER

The ocean is full of secrets and wonders.

Scan the QR code to unlock the enchanting video trailer and journey with the sisters.

TEACHER'S GUIDE: USING THE VIDEO TRAILER

The video trailer of Sisters of the Sea: Connected Through Bravery, Determination, and Kindness serves as a powerful visual and emotional entry point into the story, capturing the attention of both children and adults while introducing themes such as courage/bravery, determination/perseverance, and kindness.

As the trailer plays, the children will watch as the two sisters face challenges, learn to overcome them, and discover that their differences can unite them.

- Pause the video at key moments and ask:
- "What do you think connects the sisters besides family?"
- "What kind of bravery or determination might they need?"
- "What does bravery look like for you at school or home?"
- "How do you think kindness plays a role in this story?"

Encourage the children to share their initial reactions and predictions based on the imagery and tone of the trailer. Discussing the trailer builds anticipation and emotional investment, motivating the child to dive deeper into the story.

Consider building an "I Wonder Wall" where children's questions or predictions can be written after watching the trailer and revisited after the story unfolds.

WELCOME TO THE LEARNING GUIDE

Stories hold the power of magic and imagination as a child develops. Stories help children understand and explore their emotions, recognize relationships, and begin to see themselves in the world. When a child connects with characters in a book, they are engaging with feelings, questions, and dreams.

In *Sisters of the Sea*, themes of courage, kindness, celebrating differences, and emotional strength are gently introduced through the magic of mermaids and sisterly love: one of sunlight, one of moonlight.

The learning guide draws from holistic principles of social-emotional learning (SEL) and trauma-informed educational practices are presented in a child-friendly and creative way.

While no outside sources were directly quoted or reproduced, this work was lovingly influenced by:

- Nature-based storytelling traditions
- Bibliotherapy strategies used in mental wellness support
- Core SEL concepts from programs such as CASEL (Collaborative for Academic, Social, and Emotional Learning)
- The healing and imaginative powers of creative play

We created this book and its accompanying resources with deep respect for educators, caregivers, counselors, and families who nurture children with love, patience, and inspiration. The following learning activities and discussion prompts aim to make Storytime an enjoyable and engaging space for social-emotional growth, whether at home, in the classroom, or during quiet moments of reflection.

SOCIAL EMOTIONAL LEARNING ACTIVITIES

1. My Superpower Under the Sea

Focus: Self-Awareness, Self-Confidence, Relationship Building, and Self-Expression through drawing and writing

Instructions: Imagine you are a magical mermaid or an ocean friend! Do you have a special gift or superpower that helps others? Draw a picture of yourself in your underwater world using your superpower to help someone. Then write (or tell another student, friend, parent, or teacher) one sentence about what your power is and how it helps.

Supplies Needed:

- A printable worksheet or plain paper
- Crayons, colored pencils, or markers
- Pencils or pens
- (Optional) Glitter glue or metallic crayons for "magic effects."
- (Optional) Stickers or seashell cutouts for decoration

2. Try Again! A Mermaid Movement Game

Movement-based Activity-Focus: Self-Management, Self-Awareness, Social Awareness, Confidence-building, and Joy.

Instructions: Just like Queen in our story, let us try our best and keep going— the whole time the music plays!

Let us twirl, balance, and dance through the sea like joyful mermaids or mermen. If we fumble, that is okay! We can smile, try again, and cheer for our friends when they try too, because when we remember the magic of YET, we power up our bravery and improve our skills.

Supplies Needed:

- An open safe space (indoors or outdoors)
- Music player or sea-themed playlist (for Bluetooth connection)
- Pre-written movement cards (spin, twirl, balance, wiggle, float)
- (Optional) Mermaid tail scarves or ribbons
- (Optional) Printable "Magical YET" badge or stickers to celebrate bravery and confidence-building.

3. Light and Shadow Reflection Page

Focus: Social Awareness, Self-Awareness, and Self-Acceptance

Instructions: Everyone has parts of themselves that are bright like the sun, and quiet like the moon. Both are beautiful! In the mermaid shapes, color one to show your "sunlight" side and one to show your "shadow" side. Then draw or write what you like about each side of YOU. Both our light and shadow sides have a purpose in the emotions we express and future development. You are special in every way—light, shadow, and everything in between.

Supplies Needed:

- Printable coloring page worksheet with two mermaid outlines
- Crayons, colored pencils, or markers (choose light and dark shades)
- Pencils or pens for writing/dictating
- (Optional) Pastel chalks or watercolors to add light/dark contrast

4. Design a Coral Castle (Group Work Project)

Focus: Self-Management, Responsible Decision-Making, Social Awareness, Relationship Building, Communication Skill-building, and an opportunity to practice patience.

Instructions: Work together like the sisters in the story! Your team will design and build a beautiful coral castle where everyone feels happy and safe. Talk to each other, share ideas, and make choices together. Use your kind words and helpful hands to create something wonderful together.

Supplies Needed:

- A large sheet of poster paper or a cardboard base
- Construction paper, tissue paper, or foam sheets
- Glue sticks, child-safe scissors, and tape
- Crayons or markers for adding details.
- (Optional) Recyclable materials (toilet paper rolls = towers!)
- (Optional) Seashells, aquarium gravel, or sequins for decoration

5. Mermaid Emotion Match Game Overview

Focus: Self-Management, Responsible Decision Making, Emotion identification, Social Awareness, Memory, and Concentration focus

- **How It Works:** Create a set of **emotion cards** featuring: Mermaid faces, emojis, or scenes showing various feelings. Also, create a matching card that corresponds to the description of the event associated with the feeling.

SAMPLE PLAY IDEAS

1. **Memory Match** – Flip cards over and take turns trying to match the face with the correct word. An alternative activity -make two sets of cards with faces and feelings on the same card.
2. **Feelings Charades** – Draw a mermaid face card and act it out!
3. **Discussion Prompts** – "Have you ever felt this way? What helped you feel better?

Mermaid Emotion Card	Description or Scene
😊 Happy	Queen is practicing her dancing
😔 Sad	Queen flops as she practices her dance
😨 Scared	Queen loses her ability to swim
😍 Proud	Queen is cheering for Vampire
🥰 Loving	Sisters hugging
😎 Brave	Vampire entering the pageant
😪 Tired	Resting in the Coral Castle

Mermaid Emotion Card	Description or Scene
🤩 Excited	Preparing for the pageant
🤔 Curious	Exploring the potion ingredients

Supplies Needed:

- **Cardstock** (white or pastel for printing cards)
- **Color printer** (for full-color visuals)
- **Scissors or paper cutter**
- **Laminator and laminating sheets** (optional for reuse)
- **Velcro dots or magnets** (for interactive use on boards)

6. Ocean Mood Jar Craft

Objective: Social Awareness, connect feelings with visuals through color psychology. Students create ocean-themed jars representing emotions using layered materials and calming colors.

Instructions: Have students fill a small jar (a real jar or a jar drawn on paper) with layered colors representing different emotions in the story (e.g., dark blue for fear, gold for joy). Have them explain their color choices and when those emotions occurred in the story.

Supplies Needed:

- Clear plastic or glass jars with lids (4–8 oz size is ideal; plastic recommended for young children)

- Colored construction paper or tissue paper to represent various feelings (Layered inside the jar)
- Fine glitter or mica powder (optional: silver, blue, teal for "sea sparkle" effect)
- Small shells, beads, or sequins (optional-represent thoughts or emotions)
- Mini stickers (optional—fish, mermaids, sea stars)

SISTERS OF THE SEA: SING-ALONG SONGS

Vampire's Moonbeam Song:

Moonbeams dance on the deep, deep sea,

They shine their light and sing to me,

Guiding my heart where dreams can be.

Moonbeams dance on the deep, deep sea,

Queen's Sunshine Song:

Sunshine sparkles on coral bright,

It warms my heart and feels so light,

Calling me out to dance in the light.

Sunshine sparkles on coral bright,

Moon/Sun Final Duet Song:

Moonbeams dance on the deep, deep sea,

Sunshine sparkles on coral bright,

Together we shine in the ocean's light.

ABOUT THE AUTHOR

Annabelle Reeves is a 6-year-old author in the making who lives near the sea with her family. She loves mermaids, singing and dancing, playdates with her friends, her kitten named Pennywise, some spiders and snakes—and she imagines becoming a veterinarian in the future.

Her magical imagination shines through every page of this story, reminding us that bravery, creativity, and kindness can light up even the deepest part of the ocean.

CO-AUTHOR

Deborah Reeves (Toto Debbie) is Annabelle's grandmother, a Licensed Clinical Social Worker, a Certified Aromatherapy Professional, and a blessed grandmother who loves all her grandchildren.

She encourages creativity, connection, self-awareness, and self-expression through healing arts and storytelling. Together with Annabelle, she co-created this book as a celebration of family, imagination, a belief in magic, a reminder to follow your dreams, and an encouragement to always believe in yourself.